BEN'S MAGIC

TELESCOPE

For Freddie
~ B.P.

To Georgia,
Felix and Oscar
with love
~ S.B. & P.B.

PUFFIN BOOKS

Published by the Penguin Group
Penguin Books Ltd, 80 Strand, London WC2R 0RL, England
Penguin Putnam Inc., 375 Hudson Street, New York, New York 10014, USA
Penguin Books Australia Ltd, 250 Camberwell Road, Camberwell, Victoria 3124, Australia
Penguin Books Canada Ltd, 10 Alcorn Avenue, Toronto, Ontario, Canada M4V 3B2
Penguin Books India (P) Ltd, 11 Community Centre, Panchsheel Park, New Delhi – 110 017, India
Penguin Books (NZ) Ltd, Cnr Rosedale and Airborne Roads, Albany, Auckland, New Zealand
Penguin Books (South Africa) (Pty) Ltd, 24 Sturdee Avenue, Rosebank 2196, South Africa

Penguin Books Ltd, Registered Offices: 80 Strand, London WC2R 0RL, England

www.penguin.com

First published in hardback 2003
Published in paperback 2003
1 3 5 7 9 10 8 6 4 2

Text copyright © Brian Patten, 2003
Illustrations copyright © Siân and Peter Bailey, 2003
All rights reserved

The moral right of the author and illustrators has been asserted

Set in Monotype Baskerville

Made and printed in China

British Library Cataloguing in Publication Data
A CIP catalogue record for this book is available from the British Library

ISBN 0–140–56807–7

BEN'S MAGIC

TELESCOPE

WRITTEN BY BRIAN PATTEN

Illustrated by Siân & Peter Bailey

PUFFIN BOOKS

Ben lived on the nineteenth floor of an old tower block in a large, ugly city. From his window all he could see were factories and other tower blocks. He was bored with the same view day after day, and he wished something wonderful could happen to him. Something different. Something unexpected.

And because he made his wish on exactly the ninth hour of the ninth day of the ninth month in the ninth year of his life, something did happen.

On the ninth floor landing of the tower block, among discarded takeaway cartons and other rubbish, Ben found a silver telescope. On it were carved tiny images of the sun and moon and, between them, the image of an open eye. He took the strange telescope to his room and, standing at his window, looked through it.

In the narrow gap between the
tower blocks he saw the street
market where his mother did
her shopping. Not only that, he
could see raindrops glistening on
the covers of each separate stall.

He could hardly believe how
powerful the telescope was.

The oranges and apples, the peaches and the plums, all glowed with wonderful colours. He could see the tiny bumps on the oranges, and the bruises on the apples looked like purple maps. The more carefully he looked, the clearer everything became.

On the Indian lady's stall were rolls of bright fabric, and he could see each different coloured thread. On a stall selling household goods he could even see the reflections of people in the drinking glasses and in the pots and pans.

Ben swung the telescope around
from one side of the city to the other.
What he was seeing was the world
he lived in day after day, only now
he could see it more clearly, and it
astonished him.

On a factory wall he saw
A poor cat lick its injured paw.

He saw an old man bending down
To plant his carefully gathered seeds,
And on the track beside him grew
A multitude of flowering weeds.

He saw a dragonfly on a pond
With cathedral windows for each wing.
He saw the red tongue of a wren
when it opened up its beak to sing.

He saw sunlight tangled in a web
And a grey spider weaving gold.
Through the telescope he saw
A mayfly in a day grow old.

Ben adjusted the telescope. Now he could
see across the ocean to a world of snow
and glittering ice.

Out on the earth's cold rim he spied
Small as a handkerchief, a sail,
And like a fountain in the waves
Spume rising from the humpbacked whale.

He saw the ten billion different shapes
Made by each fleck of falling snow,
And between towering blocks of ice
He saw a double rainbow glow.

He saw saxifrages absorb the heat
Of sunlight falling on that snow,
And an inch beneath the frozen ice
He saw the winter snowbells grow.

Once again Ben adjusted the telescope.
He was back in his own country now,
watching as the daylight gave way to dusk.

He saw the owl's eye draw each ray
Of light remaining from the day,
And from its nest among the rye
He saw the field mouse sneaking by.

Then in the hollow of a tree
He saw the foxfire fungus glow.
The owl turned its head and watched
As a badger snuffled and passed below.

Ben saw the night beetle buzz about
As if dancing to the nightjar's tune,
And on its shiny back he saw
A clear reflection of the moon.

In the moon's craters his telescope caught
The footsteps of an astronaut.

Then through the telescope Ben saw
How planets roamed above the earth,
And he saw the glittering stars to which
The night itself had given birth.

Ben felt exhausted and full to
the brim with seeing so many
miraculous things. Carefully,
he put the telescope away in his
desk and looked back outside.
The tower blocks and factories
were still there, but now he
knew that beyond them was a
whole new world waiting
to be discovered.

Ben would never see the world

the same way again.

Did you see ... glistening raindrops ... stars ... an iceberg ... a centipede ... mountains ... a bicycle ... a pram ... snowflakes ... a badger ... a tiny grey mouse ... snails with stripy shells ... the moon ... a wheelbarrow ... a polar bear ... plant pots ... moonrocks ... a dragonfly ... a waterlily ... tall chimneys ... a red sail ... a garden fork ... a dog ... a grey spider ... a row of toy monkeys ... a toy rocking horse ... a fieldmouse ... a cat ... bruises on apples ... toadstools ... an upturned bath ... a fox ... the setting sun ... an astronaut's footprint ... a double rainbow ... an embroidered elephant ... a silver telescope?